June 2006

To our darling Kalia (10mths)
We hope you enjoy this book.
You are so special to us & we love
You with all our heart.
You are truly wonderful.
With love always
Mummy & Daddy xx

MR.MEN
and
little Miss

EGMONT
We bring stories to life

Illustrated by Adam Hargreaves

MR. MEN and LITTLE MISS™ & © 2005 The Hargreaves Organisation.

Printed and published under licence from Price Stern Sloan Inc., Los Angeles

First published in Great Britain in 2001.
This edition published in Great Britain in 2005 by Dean, an imprint of Egmont Books Limited,
239 Kensington High Street, London W8 6SA.

Printed and bound in Thailand
ISBN 0 603 56216 7

1 3 5 7 9 10 8 6 4 2

Roger Hargreaves' Mr Men and Little Miss characters are loved by children across the world. In this unique treasury there are twenty Mr Men and Little Miss stories featuring all your favourite original characters in some exciting and unexpected adventures! True to tradition, the stories in this book are easy to read out loud to younger children, while the bold, brightly illustrated pages are fun for older children to enjoy alone. This is a timeless collection that your child will always treasure.

This book belongs to

....

....

The MR. MEN and little Miss Treasury

by Roger Hargreaves

Contents

MR. TICKLE
in a tangle

Mr Tickle's long arms come in very handy

- most of the time!

But imagine what trouble they cause

when they're not tickling!

Now, who does that extraordinarily long arm belong to?

Of course! Mr Tickle.

And Mr Tickle's long, long arms come in very handy.

They can reach kites caught in trees.

They can answer the phone when Mr Tickle is in the bath.

But, most importantly, they are splendidly perfect for tickling!

Tickling people round corners.

Tickling people through upstairs windows.

And even tickling people on the other side of letter boxes!

However, there are days when those extraordinarily long arms are not so handy.

Days when they are nothing but a nuisance.

Days like last Monday.

Mr Tickle was lying in bed eating breakfast when he heard his garden gate open.

It was Mr Stamp, the postman.

Quick as a flash Mr Tickle sent one of his long arms down the stairs to tickle Mr Stamp.

Or, that is what he intended to do, but somehow or other, his arm got tangled up in the banisters.

Poor Mr Tickle!

It took him an hour to untangle his arm!

The letter Mr Stamp had delivered was an invitation from Mr Uppity, for lunch at the Grand Hotel.

Mr Tickle took the bus to town and sat on the upper deck.

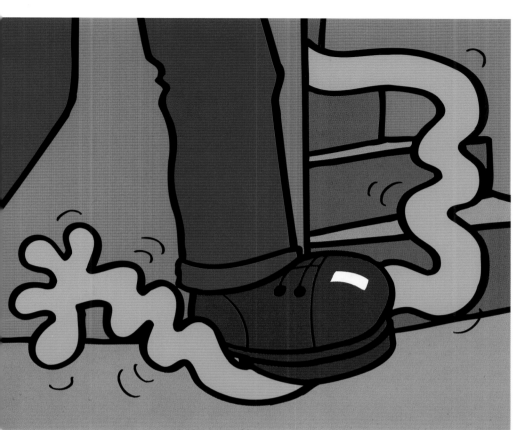

Mr Tickle sent one of his long arms down the stairs to tickle the bus driver, but, somehow or other, the ticket inspector trod on his arm!

OUCH!

Mr Tickle arrived at the Grand Hotel and rushed through the revolving door.

Or rather he tried to, but, somehow or other, his arms caught in the door.

The fire brigade had to be called out to untangle his arms, by which time he had missed lunch.

Poor Mr Tickle.

No lunch, and even worse, no tickles!

It was a very sad Mr Tickle who set off for home.

Suddenly he heard something.

He stopped. Somebody was approaching from around the corner.

Mr Tickle smiled to himself.

And sent both his arms around the corner to tickle that somebody.

But that somebody was Little Miss Naughty.

And she tied those extraordinarily long arms together in a knot!

When he got home Mr Tickle fell back into his armchair.

What a terrible day.

Not one tickle!

Suddenly there was a knock at the door.

It was Little Miss Tiny.

Mr Tickle stretched out one of his extraordinarily long arms.

Well, one tickle was better than none.

Even if it was only a tiny tickle!

LITTLE MISS SUNSHINE
keeps her smile

Little Miss Sunshine and Mr Grumpy

couldn't be more different!

But can Mr Grumpy change

Little Miss Sunshine's happy mood?

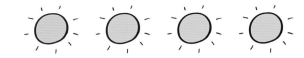

Little Miss Sunshine lives in Rise and Shine Cottage on the bank of a river.

And Little Miss Sunshine, as her name suggests, is a very happy person.

The sort of person who never gets in a bad mood.

The sort of person who is the exact opposite of somebody else who appears in this story.

That somebody is Mr Grumpy.

And Mr Grumpy, as his name suggests, is the grumpiest person in the world.

The sort of person who is always in a bad mood.

Everything annoys him.

Flowers growing in his garden. Sunny days ... and rainy days. But the thing that puts Mr Grumpy in the worst possible mood is seeing other people happy.

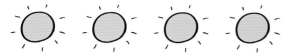 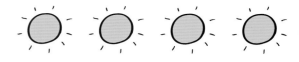

One morning Mr Grumpy met Little Miss Sunshine.

"Good morning, Mr Grumpy," said Miss Sunshine cheerfully.

"There's nothing good about it," snapped Mr Grumpy.

"Humph," huffed Mr Grumpy, after Miss Sunshine had left.
"That Miss Sunshine is always so abominably happy!
Just for once I'd like to see her in a bad mood."

It was on his way home that Mr Grumpy thought of a plan. A plan to upset Little Miss Sunshine.

He raced home and made a list of all the things that were guaranteed to upset him.

It was a very long list!

"Now, there must be something here that will put Miss Sunshine in a bad mood," he said to himself.

Mr Grumpy was not a very nice man!

The first thing Mr Grumpy had written on his list was, 'waiting for buses'.

So the next day Mr Grumpy opened a gate and let all Farmer Fields' sheep out into the lane! And the bus was delayed for hours and hours while all the sheep were rounded up.

Mr Grumpy ran round to the bus stop.

"Tee hee," he chuckled nastily, "I can't wait to see how upset Miss Sunshine is."

But Little Miss Sunshine was not upset.

In fact she was not there.

It was such a nice day she had decided to walk into town.

"Bother!" said Mr Grumpy.

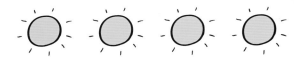

The next day Mr Grumpy looked at the second thing on the list.

'Losing', he read out loud.

So that evening he invited Miss Sunshine round to his house to play cards and … he cheated!

But Little Miss Sunshine, being the happy-go-lucky person she is, did not mind losing.

Mr Grumpy won every game they played.

"Oh, well played, Mr Grumpy," she said at the end of the evening.

"Drat and bother," said Mr Grumpy after she had left.

 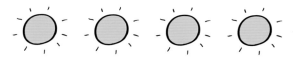

Mr Grumpy read down his list again.

Number three said, 'getting caught in the rain'.

Mr Grumpy filled up his watering can and, using his ladder, climbed a tree just outside Miss Sunshine's house.

And there he waited until Miss Sunshine came out for her walk.

But Little Miss Sunshine saw the ladder.

"What a silly place to leave a ladder," she said to herself, and walked round the other side of the tree and put the ladder away.

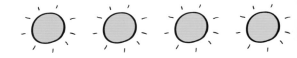
"Drat, bother and blast," muttered Mr Grumpy, who ended up stuck in the tree all night.

Well, nearly all night. Just before sunrise he fell asleep … and fell out of the tree!

The fourth thing on Mr Grumpy's list was 'queues'.

Mr Grumpy waited until Little Miss Sunshine went shopping and then he rushed ahead of her to the greengrocer's. Where he started an argument with Mrs Pod about the quality of her peas.

As he argued a queue began to grow behind him and when he glanced back he saw Miss Sunshine standing at the back of the queue.

Mr Grumpy was furious.

But then he met Mr Nosey and had another thoroughly nasty idea.

"Do you know," said Mr Grumpy, "what Little Miss Sunshine calls Miss Bossy behind her back? She calls her knobbly knees!"

Mr Grumpy's thoroughly nasty idea was to start a rumour that would get Little Miss Sunshine into trouble.

He smiled to himself and carried on arguing until he felt sure she must be fed up of waiting.

But when he turned round the queue had disappeared and when he went outside he found everyone in the queue happily chatting with Little Miss Sunshine.

"Double drat, bother and blast!"

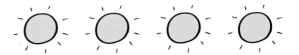 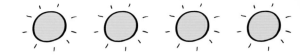

And the rumour spread.

Mr Nosey told Little Miss Star who told Mr Uppity who told Little Miss Splendid ... who told Mr Muddle ... who told Little Miss Bossy.

"... and Little Miss Sunshine said that Mr Grumpy calls you knobbly knees," said Mr Muddle.

"Did he now!" said Miss Bossy, grimly, and marched straight round to Mr Grumpy's house and punched him on the nose!

It was a very sorry-looking Mr Grumpy that Little Miss Sunshine met outside her house the next day.

Miss Sunshine invited him in for breakfast to cheer him up and cooked him fried eggs.

Sunny side up, of course!

And did she manage to cheer up Mr Grumpy?

 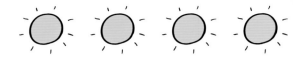

Of course not!

No more than Mr Grumpy can upset Little Miss Sunshine!

MR. HAPPY
finds a hobby

Lots of the Mr Men have hobbies.
But do you think Mr Happy can find
the right hobby for Mr Grumble?

Mr Happy is a happy sort of fellow.

He lives in Happyland, which is a happy sort of place.

Behind his house there is a wood full of happy birds and on the other side of the wood there is a lake full of happy fish.

Now, one day, not that long ago, Mr Happy went for a walk down through the wood.

As he came to the shore of the lake he heard an unusual sound.

A sound that is seldom heard in Happyland. It was the sound of somebody moaning and grumbling.

Mr Happy peered round the trunk of a tree.

At the edge of the lake there was somebody fishing.

Fishing and grumbling.

And grumbling and fishing.

It was Mr Grumble.

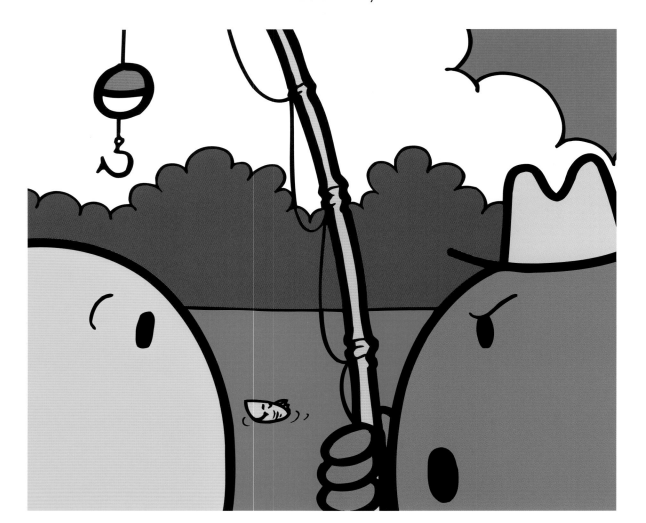

"Good morning, Mr Grumble," said Mr Happy.

"Ssssh!" ssshed Mr Grumble.

"Sorry," whispered Mr Happy. "Have you caught anything?"

"Yes! I've caught a cold!" grumbled Mr Grumble.

"I've been sitting here all night. I hate fishing!"

"Then, why *are* you fishing?" asked Mr Happy.

"Because Mr Quiet said it was fun! And, you see, I'm trying to find something I enjoy doing. Something I can do as a hobby."

"Hmmm," pondered Mr Happy. "I might be able to help. Come on, let's see if we can find you a hobby."

As they walked along, Mr Happy thought long and hard, and as he thought, Mr Grumble grumbled.

He grumbled about the noise the birds were making.

He grumbled about having to walk.

But most of all he grumbled about not having a hobby.

Grumble, grumble, grumble.

First of all they met Mr Rush in his car. Mr Happy explained what they were doing.

"What's your hobby?" asked Mr Grumble.

"Speed!" said Mr Rush.

"Hop in!" And they did.

Mr Grumble very quickly decided that he did not like going fast.

Next they met Little Miss Giggles.

"What's your hobby?" asked Mr Grumble.

"I ... tee hee ... like ... tee hee ... giggling," giggled Miss Giggles.

So they went to the circus to see the clowns.

Little Miss Giggles giggled, Mr Happy laughed and

Mr Grumble ... frowned!

"I hate custard pies," grumbled Mr Grumble.

It proved to be a very long day for Mr Happy.

They went everywhere.

They went to Little Miss Splendid's house.

But Mr Grumble did not like hats.

They went to Mr Mischief's house.

But Mr Grumble did not like practical jokes.

39

They bounced with Mr Bounce.

And they looked through keyholes with Mr Nosey.

But nothing was right.
In fact, nothing was left.

Mr Happy had run out of ideas.

As the sun was setting they
saw Mr Impossible coming
towards them down the lane.

"Now, if anybody can help us that somebody ought to be Mr Impossible," said Mr Happy.

"Hello," he said. "You're good at the impossible. Can you think of a hobby that Mr Grumble would enjoy?"

"That ..." said Mr Impossible.
"Yes ..." said Mr Happy and Mr Grumble together.
"... would be impossible," said Mr Impossible.
"Grrr!" growled Mr Grumble, and stomped off home.

It was while drinking a cup of tea the next morning that Mr Happy had an idea. A perfectly obvious idea.

He rushed round to Mr Grumble's house.

"I've got it!" cried Mr Happy. "You can take up fishing."

"Fishing!? But I hate fishing."

"I know, but what do you do while you are fishing?" asked Mr Happy.

"I don't know."

"You grumble," said Mr Happy. "And what do you like doing most of all?"

"I like …" and then it dawned on Mr Grumble. "I like grumbling!"

Mr Grumble looked at Mr Happy and then, for the first time in a very long time, he smiled.

A very small smile, but
a smile all the same.

LITTLE MISS TROUBLE
moving house

Little Miss Trouble has decided
to move house.
Which means one thing for her
new neighbours - Trouble!

Little Miss Trouble lives in Uptonogood Cottage, surrounded by fields and trees and more fields and more trees and even more fields.

Her nearest neighbours live miles and miles away and there is a very good reason for this.

That very good reason is Miss Trouble!

Nobody wants to live next door to somebody who causes so much trouble.

Somebody who telephoned Mr Lazy at 5 o'clock every morning for a whole week.

And somebody who told Mr Wrong that the best thing to use to polish his car was boot polish.

Now, because she lived all on her own, Miss Trouble found that she could not cause half as much trouble as she would like to.

What Little Miss Trouble longed for more than anything else was a neighbour.

One Monday, when Little Miss Trouble was walking in the woods near her house, she came upon a wishing-well.

"Well, I never," she said, and then she had an idea. She threw a coin in the well.

"I wish I lived next door to … somebody," she said out loud.

The next morning, when she looked out of her window, she discovered that, as if by magic, which it was, her house was next door to Box Cottage, which is where Mr Chatterbox lives.

"Tee hee, now for some fun!" giggled Miss Trouble.

She crept down the lane, around the corner, up a telegraph pole and cut the telephone line!

Poor Mr Chatterbox.

No telephone.

No one to chat to.

But it was then that he looked out the window and saw
Miss Trouble's house.

Five minutes later there was a knock at Little Miss Trouble's door.

"Hello," said Mr Chatterbox. "Just thought I'd pop round for a
quick chat. Funny thing, you know, my telephone's broken and … "

And Mr Chatterbox talked and chatted and chatted and talked
through the morning, all afternoon and late into the night.

The next day, Tuesday, a very tired Little Miss Trouble went back to the wishing-well and threw in another coin. "I wish that I lived next door to someone else," she said.

And the very next morning Little Miss Trouble found herself living next door to Mr Bump.

She threw a brick through one of his windows, but Mr Bump has so many accidents that he did not notice one more broken window.

Little Miss Trouble went back to the wishing-well.

On Wednesday Miss Trouble tried to play a trick on Little Miss Lucky. But she discovered that Little Miss Lucky is too lucky for any of Miss Trouble's tricks to work on her.

On Thursday there was nobody in at Little Miss Late's house.

She was late getting back from her holiday!

On Friday Little Miss Trouble told Mr Muddle that Mr Small had called him an egghead.

But Mr Muddle got muddled up, and instead of being angry with Mr Small he thanked him!

On Saturday Little Miss Trouble let the tyres down on Mr Forgetful's car.

But Mr Forgetful forgot he had a car and caught the bus.

On Sunday it was a very fed-up Little Miss Trouble who returned to the wishing-well to make a wish.

And then she had a thought.

A thought that went like this, "The trouble with neighbours," thought Little Miss Trouble, "is that they are too much trouble!"

And she went home and was very, very good and didn't make any trouble for anybody for ever and ever …

... well, until Tuesday!

MR. SILLY
gets the giggles

Lots of silly things happen

in Nonsenseland.

So what could possibly give

Mr Silly the giggles?

Mr Silly lives in a place called Nonsenseland where the grass is blue and the trees are red. Which you already know.

It is also a place where zebra crossings are spotty. Which you probably did not know.

In Nonsenseland you post letters in telephone boxes and you make phone calls from letter boxes.

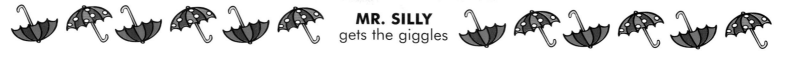

And in Nonsenseland the umbrellas all have holes in them so that you know when it has stopped raining.

Which is utter nonsense, but not if your name is Mr Silly.

Now, one morning last week, Mr Silly got up, put on his hat, brushed his teeth with soap, as usual, polished his shoes with toothpaste, as usual, and went down to breakfast.

For breakfast, Mr Silly had fried eggs and custard, as usual, and a cup of hot, milky marmalade, as usual.

After breakfast he went out into his garden. The day before, Mr Silly had bought a tree, but as he looked at the tree he realised that he did not have a hole to plant it in.

So he went to the hardware shop.

"Good morning," said Mr Silly. "I would like to buy a hole."

"Sorry," said the sales assistant," we're all out of holes. Sold the last one yesterday."

"Bother," said Mr Silly.

He decided there was nothing for it but to go in search of a hole.

He walked and he walked and he walked.

Eventually Mr Silly stopped walking and looked down at his feet.

"That's odd," he said, "this grass is green."

"Of course it is," said a voice behind him. "Grass is always green."

"Who are you?" asked Mr Silly.

"Little Miss Wise."

"I'm Mr Silly. Could you tell me where I am?"

"You're in Sensibleland," said Miss Wise.

Mr Silly had walked so far that he had walked right out of Nonsenseland.

"I'm looking for a hardware shop," said Mr Silly. "Can you help?"

"Certainly," said Miss Wise. "Follow me."

As they walked along Mr Silly looked around.

He had never seen anywhere like it. The grass was green, the trees were green, even the hedges were green.

They came to a zebra crossing. A stripy zebra crossing.

Mr Silly chuckled, and then he giggled and then he laughed out loud.

"Why are you laughing?" asked Miss Wise.

"The … hee hee … zebra crossing … ha ha … is stripy," laughed Mr Silly.

"What else would a zebra crossing be?" said Miss Wise.

"Spotty, of course!" said Mr Silly, wiping the tears from his eyes.

"How silly," said Miss Wise.

They set off again and the further they went the more Mr Silly laughed.

He laughed when he saw someone posting a letter in a letter box.

He laughed when he saw someone using a phone in a telephone box.

And he laughed when he saw an umbrella without holes in it.

65

Eventually they came to Miss Bolt's Hardware Shop.

"Good afternoon," said Mr Silly. "I would like to buy a hole."

"A hole?" questioned Miss Bolt.

"Yes, big enough to plant a tree in," explained Mr Silly.

Miss Bolt sniggered. Miss Wise chortled.

And then they burst out laughing.

"I've never heard anything so absurd," laughed Miss Bolt.

"But I do have something that may help."

That evening Mr Silly invited his friend Mr Nonsense for supper and told him all about his day in Sensibleland.

Mr Nonsense laughed so hard he fell off his chair!

"… and then," continued Mr Silly, "Miss Privet gave me a spade. A spade! Why in the world would I want to buy a spade when all I wanted was a hole!"

"Hee hee … that's … ha ha … ridiculous!" laughed Mr Nonsense.

"What's for pudding?"

"Spam roly-poly," answered Mr Silly.

"Oh, goody," said Mr Nonsense. "My favourite."

LITTLE MISS SCATTERBRAIN
sets off for the sun

Little Miss Scatterbrain's friends help her

plan a holiday in the sun.

Now what could possibly go wrong ...?

Little Miss Scatterbrain

is the sort of person who gets everything mixed up.

Like the morning she hung slices of bread from the washing line and put her handkerchiefs in the bread bin.

Like the afternoon she vacuumed the lawn and mowed the carpets.

And like the evening when she wanted to watch her favourite television programme, but turned on the radio instead.

Little Miss Scatterbrain is so scatterbrained that she forgets where her own front door is! Have you ever heard of anything so scatterbrained?

This story is about the time that she went on her summer holiday.

Little Miss Scatterbrain, as you can imagine, is not very good at organising holidays.

The year before last she went skiing, but ended up on the beach!

And last year she went camping and packed an electric kettle!

This year she was determined that nothing would go wrong.

And to make sure that nothing did go wrong she asked her friends to help her.

Mr Clever helped to book her summer holiday.

Little Miss Splendid helped her shop for her holiday.

Little Miss Tidy helped her pack.

Mr Rush took her to the station.

And Mr Strong carried her luggage onto the train.

Nothing could go wrong. Or that's what Little Miss Scatterbrain thought.

However, something did go wrong.

And that something was Little Miss Scatterbrain getting off at the wrong station.

She crossed the road and went into the hotel opposite the station.

"Good morning," she said, even though it was the afternoon, "my name is Miss Scatterbrain."

The hotel manager looked down his list of guests, but there was no booking in her name.

And of course there wouldn't be.

Little Miss Scatterbrain was in the wrong town. And because she was in the wrong town, she had to be in the wrong hotel.

"That's odd," she said, as she came out of the hotel. "Never mind, I'll go down to the beach."

She asked the next person she met where the beach was.

"Sorry, there's no beach here," came the reply.

"That's odd," she said, for the second time that day.

As she stood in the street wondering what to do somebody else walked by and said, "Looks like snow."

Miss Scatterbrain looked up at the sky and as she did, a large snowflake floated down and landed on her nose.

"That's odd," she said, for the third time that day.

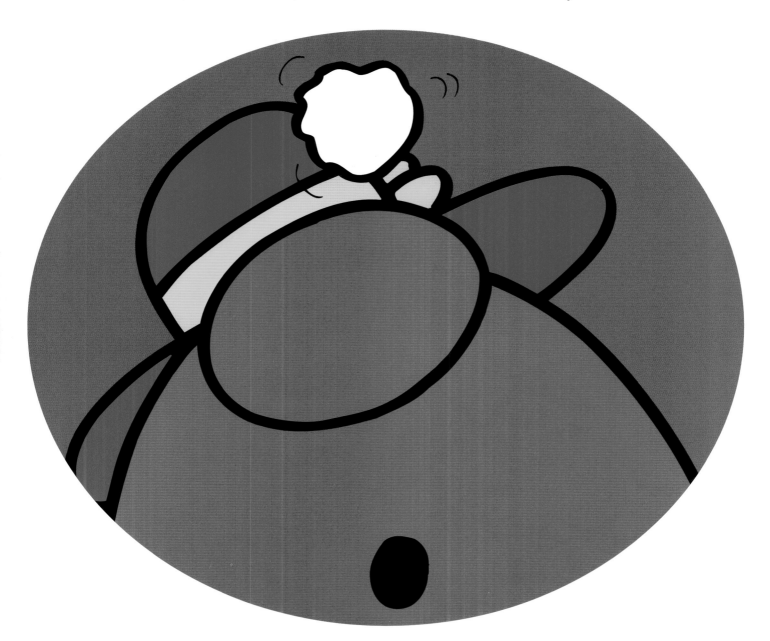

A week later, back from her holiday, Little Miss Scatterbrain met Mr Clever.

"Hello," said Mr Clever. "Did you enjoy your holiday?"

"Yes," said Miss Scatterbrain, "do you want to see my photos?" And she showed Mr Clever her holiday snaps.

Not surprisingly, Mr Clever was rather surprised.

"That's odd. Where did you go?" he asked.

"It began with an 'S'," said Miss Scatterbrain.

"I know. I booked it for you," said Mr Clever. "You went to Seatown."

"No," said Miss Scatterbrain, "Hmmmm, let me think, oh, I know, it was Shivertown!"

"I should have guessed," smiled Mr Clever.

"By the way, did you get my postcard?"

"No, but I did get your postcard meant for Miss Splendid," chuckled Mr Clever.

"That's odd," said Miss Scatterbrain.

But I don't think there's anything odd about that, do you?

MR. BUMP
loses his memory

This time Mr Bump has bumped
his head once too often!
Find out what happens when he starts
to believe he is really Mr Careful!

Mr Bump is the
sort of person
who is always
having accidents.

Small accidents.

Medium-sized

accidents.

And big accidents.

Lots and lots

of accidents.

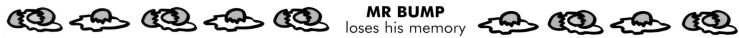

One day Mr Bump got out of bed, or rather, he fell out of bed, as he did every morning.

He drew back the curtains and opened the window.

It was a beautiful day.

He leant on the windowsill and breathed in deeply and ... fell out of the window.

BUMP!

Mr Bump sat up and rubbed his head. And as he rubbed,
it dawned on him that he had no idea where he was.

He had no idea whose garden he was sitting in.

He had no idea whose house he was sitting in front of.

And he had no
idea who he was.

Mr Bump had
lost his memory.

Mr Bump walked up to his garden gate and looked down the lane.

Mr Muddle was passing by.

"Good afternoon," said Mr Muddle.

As you and I know, it was morning. But Mr Muddle, not surprisingly, always gets things in a muddle.

"I seem to have lost my memory," said Mr Bump. "Do you know what my name is?"

"You're Mr Careful," said Mr Muddle.

"Thank you," said Mr Bump.

Mr Bump went into town.

The first person he met
was Mrs Packet the grocer,
carrying an armful
of groceries.

"Hello," said Mr Bump, "I'm
Mr Careful, can I help?"

"Just the person! I need
someone careful to deliver
these eggs."

Mr Bump took the eggs
from Mrs Packet and set
off down the High Street.

And because he was Mr
Bump he slipped and fell
on the eggs, breaking all
of them.

"You're not all that careful,
are you?" said Mrs Packet.

"Sorry," said Mr Bump.

He walked on past the dairy. Mr Bottle, the manager, came out.

"I'm looking for someone to drive the milk float," he said. "What's your name?"

"Mr Careful," replied Mr Bump.

"Perfect," said Mr Bottle. "I need someone careful to do the milk round."

Mr Bump set off down the road.

As he rounded the corner he hit the kerb and the milk float turned over, smashing all the milk bottles.

"Well, that wasn't very carefully done, was it?" said Mr Bottle.

"Sorry," said Mr Bump.

Then he met Mr Brush, the painter, who was up a ladder, painting.

"Hello," said Mr Bump. "I'm Mr Careful. Do you need a hand?"

"Yes, please," replied Mr Brush. "I need someone careful to pass up that paint pot."

Mr Bump began to climb the ladder.

And being Mr Bump, he fell off and the pot of paint landed on his head.

Mr Bump went for a walk.

"I don't understand it," he said to himself. "My name is Mr Careful, but I can't do anything carefully!"

It was then that he walked into a tree.

'BUMP!'

And bumped his head.

An apple fell out of the tree into his hand.

"That's odd," he said to himself. "How did I get here?
The last thing I remember is opening my bedroom window."

"... And where did all this paint come from?"

You know, don't you.

Just at that moment Farmer Fields turned up.

"Careful ..." he called.

"That sounds familiar," said Mr Bump,

and fell down the bank into the river.

LITTLE MISS BOSSY
and the magic word

Little Miss Bossy is just too bossy!

So Mr Small and Little Miss Magic

decide to teach her a lesson ...

Little Miss Bossy is bossy.

Bossier than the bossiest person you know.

She is also very rude.

Nearly as rude as Mr Uppity, which is very rude indeed.

She never says please.

And she never says thank you.

Like the time she met Mr Sneeze.

"ATISHOO!" sneezed Mr Sneeze.

"Stop sneezing!" ordered Miss Bossy.

"I can't, ATISHOO!, help it," replied Mr Sneeze.

"Nonsense!" said Miss Bossy.

Like the time she met Little Miss Chatterbox.

"Good morning," said Miss Chatterbox. "Lovely day, isn't it? Just the right weather for a walk. Talking about the weather …"

"Be quiet!" ordered Miss Bossy.

And like the time she tripped over Mr Small.

"You're too small!" exclaimed Miss Bossy. "Grow up!"

"I can't," said Mr Small.

"Then get out of my way in future!" ordered Miss Bossy.

Poor Mr Sneeze.

Poor Little Miss Chatterbox.

And poor Mr Small.

It was Mr Small who decided that something had to be done.

He went to see Little Miss Magic.

And once he had explained the problem she agreed to teach Miss Bossy a lesson.

"... and I think I know just how to do it," she replied.

The next day Little Miss Bossy bumped into Mr Greedy.

"You're too big," she cried. "Lose some weight!"

At the same time Little Miss Magic, who had followed Miss Bossy, muttered a very magic word.

And do you know what happened?

Of course you don't …

97

... but you do now!

"Who are you calling big?" laughed Mr Greedy. "You ought to take a look at yourself!"

Little Miss Bossy was lost for words.

As soon as Mr Greedy had gone Miss Magic muttered some more magic words and Miss Bossy returned to normal.

Further down the lane Miss Bossy passed Mr Cheerful's gate.

He was painting stripes on his house to cheer it up.

"That looks ridiculous," snapped Miss Bossy.

"Paint over those stripes!"

Little Miss Magic whispered the very magic word again.

Mr Cheerful started to chuckle.

"You ought to look at yourself," he laughed.

Miss Bossy did.

She was covered in stripes!

From her hiding place, Little Miss Magic smiled to herself.

Next, she met Little Miss Splendid.

"What a stupid hat," she said. "Go and put on something more sensible!"

Miss Magic uttered the magic word again and I'm sure you can guess what happened next.

"Speak for yourself!" said Miss Splendid, bursting into laughter.

And for the third time that day Little Miss Bossy was lost for words.

101

Just then Mr Small came along.

"Having a nice day?" he asked.

"Mind your own business, pip-squeak!" snapped Miss Bossy.

"And who are you to call me pip-squeak!" said Mr Small, and chuckled.

"Haven't you learnt your lesson yet?"

Miss Magic came out from behind the tree where she had been hiding.

"Oh, it's you," squeaked Miss Bossy. "Turn me back to my proper size!"

"You have to say the magic word," replied Miss Magic.

"Abracadabra," squeaked Miss Bossy.

"No, that's not the magic word I was thinking of."

I'm sure you know what the magic word is, but it took Miss Bossy
a bit longer to think of it.

"Please," she said eventually.

And did she learn her lesson?

Well, she learnt one lesson.

Little Miss Bossy is still just as bossy as ever,
but at least she now says please!

"GO TO SLEEP!"

"Please."

MR. FUNNY
upsets Mr Fussy

Mr Funny can always make people laugh.
But when he makes Mr Fussy laugh
he causes all kinds of trouble!

Mr Funny

lives in a teapot-shaped house.

He drives a shoe-shaped car.

And he has a teacup-shaped bath.

Mr Fussy lives in a very ordinary house, drives a very ordinary car and his bath is a very ordinary bath.

Mr Funny is a very funny fellow.

So funny that when he pulls one of his funny faces you can't help but laugh.

Mr Fussy is very serious.

Very serious about keeping everything neat and tidy and spick and span.

Now Mr Funny lives at the very end of Long Lane and Mr Fussy lives half-way down Long Lane.

So whenever Mr Funny goes out for a drive in his shoe car he has to pass Mr Fussy's house.

Every time that Mr Funny passes Mr Fussy he pulls one of his funny faces.

And as hard as he tries, Mr Fussy can't help laughing.

He laughs so much that he ends up having accidents.

Like the time he was mowing his lawn.

He laughed so much he ruined all his nice straight lines.

And when he was cleaning his windows.

He laughed so much he fell off his ladder and squashed his prize pumpkin.

And he burnt his shoelaces while he was ironing them.

Mr Fussy was fed up.

But then he had an idea.

He put up a sign on the lane just before his house.

It read: 'Please Beep Your Horn.'

"That should work," he said to himself.

The idea was that if Mr Funny beeped his horn Mr Fussy would have some warning and he could stop whatever it was he was doing.

The next day Mr Funny was driving down the lane as usual when he saw Mr Fussy's sign.

So he beeped his car's horn.

Now, so far Mr Fussy's idea had worked, but what he had not reckoned on was the sound that Mr Funny's car horn would make.

It doesn't go 'BEEP.'

Oh no, it sounds like somebody making a very loud raspberry noise.

'THURRRPT!' went the car horn.

Mr Fussy was outside in his coal bunker. Stacking his coal in neat rows.

Mr Fussy didn't like untidy piles of coal!

When Mr Fussy heard the sound Mr Fussy's car horn made he started to giggle.

And then he chuckled.

And then he laughed.

And he laughed so much he fell over into his neatly stacked coal.

Once he had recovered from his laughing fit he stormed out of his coal bunker.

He was covered from head to foot in coal.

And he was furious. He stormed over to Mr Funny.

"That's the most ridiculous car horn I've ever heard," he yelled at Mr Funny.

Mr Funny stopped his shoe car beside Mr Fussy's gate.

"There's a reason for that," he explained.

"It's because it's not a car horn,"

"it's a …"

" … shoe-horn, ha ha ha, hee hee hee," he laughed.

And even Mr Fussy had to admit that was quite funny.

Wouldn't you agree?

LITTLE MISS NEAT
and the last leaf

Autumn is a worrying time for
Little Miss Neat! But then along comes
Mr Happy with the perfect solution!

Little Miss Neat likes things to be neat.

Which is why she is called Little Miss Neat.

She likes things to be as neat as two new pins.

Which is why her cottage is called Two Pin Cottage.

One autumn day Little
Miss Neat looked out of
her window to admire
her very neat garden.

As she looked, a leaf
fell from the tree in the
middle of her lawn.

"Oh, goodness
gracious!" she cried.
"What a mess!"

She rushed outside,
picked up the leaf,
went back indoors
and put the leaf in her
rubbish bin.

"That's better," she said
to herself.

But when she looked out of the window again there was another leaf lying on her immaculate lawn.

Out she rushed again and picked up the leaf and put it in the bin.

And so it went on all day long.

Rushing backwards and forwards until it was too dark to
see anything.

Poor Little Miss Neat was exhausted.

"I don't like autumn," she murmured to herself as she fell asleep.

The next morning was even worse.

Little Miss Neat had to sprint to keep up with the falling leaves.

And that was how Mr Happy found her at lunchtime.

Running backwards and forwards.

"You look exhausted," said Mr Happy.

"I am," puffed Miss Neat, "but I have to pick up all these horrid, messy leaves."

"Do you know what I do?" said Mr Happy. "I wait until all the leaves have fallen and then I pick them up. You ought to try it. It's much easier."

After Mr Happy had left, Miss Neat thought about what he had said and decided she would try it.

But it was easier said than done.

Poor Little Miss Neat worried and fretted and fretted and worried as the leaves slowly covered her lawn.

She hated it.

But eventually all the leaves had fallen.

Well, nearly all the leaves.

There was just one leaf left in the tree.

Little Miss Neat waited.

And waited.

And waited.

When it got too dark to see she got a torch and waited.

And waited.

And waited.

All night long!

And that was how Mr Happy found her the next morning.

Still waiting!

"What are you doing?" asked Mr Happy.

"What you suggested I should do," replied Miss Neat. "I'm waiting for all the leaves to fall."

Mr Happy smiled, reached up and plucked the last leaf from the tree.

"Oh," said Miss Neat, suddenly feeling rather foolish.

And she blushed.

Mr Happy helped her to rake up all the leaves.

And by teatime Little Miss Neat's garden was as neat and as tidy as it usually was.

"You know what you should do next year?" said Mr Happy.

"Oh please! No more suggestions!" cried Miss Neat.

"Don't worry," said Mr Happy. "You'll like this one. I think that next year you should go on holiday and ask Mr Busy to clear up the leaves. It wouldn't take him a minute."

"What a good idea!" said Miss Neat.

"You've taken a leaf out of my book," smiled Mr Happy.

"And turned over a new leaf," chuckled Miss Neat.

"You can leaf through the holiday brochures," giggled Mr Happy.

"And I can leave the leaves behind," laughed Miss Neat.

"Hee hee, oh stop it, hee hee hee," laughed Mr Happy.

"Leaf me alone! Ha! Ha! Ha!"

MR. GREEDY

is helpfully heavy

Mr Greedy is getting heavier and heavier
which is quite a problem -
until he finds a way to put his weight
to work!

Mr Greedy likes to eat.

And the more he eats the bigger he gets, and the bigger he gets the heavier he becomes.

Which was a problem, as you will see.

Mr Greedy woke up and yawned and stretched.

'CRACK!'

'BUMP!'

The 'CRACK!' was the sound of Mr Greedy's bed breaking and the 'BUMP!' was the sound of Mr Greedy hitting the floor.

"Oh dear," said Mr Greedy.

Mr Greedy got up off the floor and went into the bathroom and ran a bath.

But when he got into the bath all the water got out.

There was not enough room in the bath for both Mr Greedy and the water!

"Oh dear," he said again.

Mr Greedy looked at himself in his mirror.

He had a wide mirror, but he was even wider and could not see very much of himself.

"Oh dear."

131

He went downstairs for breakfast.

As he waited for the bread to toast he let his hand rest on the loaf of bread.

And squashed it flat.

He even had heavy hands!

After a large breakfast of squashed toast he leant back in his chair.

There was another loud 'CRACK!' and 'BUMP!' He found himself on the floor again.

"I wish I wasn't so heavy," he sighed to himself.

Now Mr Greedy had been invited to Mr Uppity's house
for lunch.

So Mr Greedy squeezed through his front door and squeezed
into his car.

He started the engine.

Then, with four loud bangs, all four tyres on his car burst.

'BANG! BANG! BANG! BANG!'

He had to get the bus.

But when he climbed on, the other end of the bus tipped up!

"I think you need to lose some weight,"
suggested the bus conductor.

As the bus drove off without him, Mr Greedy looked down at his large tummy.

"Oh dear," he sighed, not for the first time that day.

Mr Greedy had to walk all the way to Mr Uppity's house.

He was very tired and very hot and very hungry when he got there.

Mr Uppity lived in the biggest house in Bigtown.

Mr Uppity was very rich.

Mr Uppity answered the door.

"What do you want?" he demanded.

Mr Uppity was very rude.

"You invited me for lunch," said Mr Greedy.

"Oh yes," said Mr Uppity. "You'll have to wait. I'm very busy."

"What are you doing?" asked Mr Greedy.

"Packing," answered Mr Uppity, and went up to his bedroom.

Mr Greedy followed.

Mr Uppity's bedroom was full of suitcases and every suitcase was overflowing.

Mr Uppity went round the room trying to close them, but they were so full it was impossible.

"Don't just stand there, give me a hand," ordered Mr Uppity bossily.

Mr Greedy tried pushing a suitcase shut, but it was no good.

Then he had an idea.

He sat on the lid of the suitcase, and because he was so heavy the suitcase closed.

137

"Brilliant," said Mr Uppity. "You can shut the rest."

Mr Greedy beamed.

For the first time in a very long time Mr Greedy had found something useful that he could do.

...all...d ...ppi... ...to the great
every after. The End.

when he returned he said what a lovely

Going on holiday? Having trouble fitting everything in your suitcase?

Then call ▢

Mr. Greedy.

The expert suitcase squasher.

Disaster strikes as the daisy above Mr. Small's house is blown over in high winds.

Mr. Strong breaks egg-eating record by 302 eggs. Ask how he felt he said 'very strong'.

Little Miss Bossy fell over laughing which is very unusual.

And on his way home Mr Greedy had an idea.

An idea that meant he could be useful every day.

He went to the local newspaper and placed an advertisement.

Mr Greedy had found himself a job.

He went home, ate a huge supper to celebrate, went to bed and slept.

And do you know how he slept?

I'll tell you.

He slept …

... heavily.

LITTLE MISS NAUGHTY
worries Mr Worry

Little Miss Naughty could have
much more fun if only Mr Worry
would stop worrying her.
But will he spoil her fun forever?

Little Miss Naughty

is quite the naughtiest person that I know.

Take the other day, for example.

She tied Mr Tall's shoelaces together.

And she took Mr Dizzy into the maze and left him there.

And she joined up all the dots on Miss Dotty's house.

And she even picked on the worm who lives at the bottom of her garden!

I think you would have to agree that she is probably the naughtiest person you know.

Then one day Little Miss Naughty met Mr Worry.

Now, Mr Worry is the sort of person who worries about everything.

Absolutely everything!

"Let's have some fun," suggested Miss Naughty, after they had introduced themselves.

Mr Worry was worried that if he said no he might offend Miss Naughty, so he said yes.

But he was still worried what 'fun' somebody called Miss Naughty might get up to.

And as you have seen, he was right to worry!

Miss Naughty led him to Mr Tickle's house.

"Let's ring Mr Tickle's doorbell and run away," she giggled.

"Ooh, I don't know," said Mr Worry. "Mr Tickle might be in the bath."

"Even better!" laughed Miss Naughty.

"But then he would be all wet, and he might slip, and he might fall down the stairs, and he might bump his head, and then there wouldn't be anybody to call the Doctor because we would have run away!"

Up to this point Little Miss Naughty had never worried about anything in her entire life.

But, now, when she thought about what Mr Worry had said, ringing Mr Tickle's doorbell and running away suddenly didn't seem such a good idea after all.

"Come on," she said. "I've got a better idea."

They walked over to Mr Uppity's house.

"Why don't we let his tyres down?" chuckled Little Miss Naughty.

Mr Worry looked worried.

"But what if Mr Uppity didn't notice he had flat tyres until he got out on the road, and then he might get stuck, and then a fire engine might come along, and it might not be able to get past, and then it couldn't put out the fire!" gasped Mr Worry.

147

"Oh," said Miss Naughty. "I hadn't thought of that."

She had thought of something else, though, and off they went.

But it didn't matter what she thought up, Mr Worry could think of something to worry about. Which then gave Little Miss Naughty something to worry about.

They didn't push Mr Bounce off the gate because he might have bounced up into a tree and never been able to get down.

They didn't scatter Little Miss Scatterbrain's marbles because she might have got upset if they had been lost.

Little Miss Naughty was distraught.

All those wonderful, naughty ideas going to waste.

And then she had another idea.

And tripped up Mr Worry, who fell flat on his face!

"What did you do that for?" said Mr Worry. "I might have rolled down the hill, and I might have fallen in the river, and then I might have caught a cold, and I might have had to stay in bed all week!"

Little Miss Naughty looked at Mr Worry.

"But you didn't," she said,
and ran off giggling mischievously.

MR. STRONG
and the flood

Mr Strong is beginning to wish
he wasn't quite so strong -
until he comes across a farmer
in need of help!

Mr Strong is unbelievably strong.

So strong that sometimes he forgets his own strength.

Like the other day.

It was raining.

So Mr Strong pulled on his wellington boots. But he pulled too hard and his foot went right through the bottom of his boot!

Then he went out through his front door and opened his umbrella.

But he pushed too hard and turned the umbrella inside out!

So he tried to go back inside to get another umbrella (Mr Strong gets through a lot of umbrellas) but when he turned the doorknob it came off in his hand.

Poor Mr Strong was not having a good day.

Fortunately, when you are as strong as Mr Strong you don't need a door to get inside your house.

Do you know what he did?

He picked up the corner of his house and slipped in under the wall!

Once he had fetched a new umbrella and opened it (very carefully this time) and opened his door (very carefully) he set off for his walk.

Now as you might remember I mentioned that it was raining.

What I did not tell you was that it had been raining for days and days and days.

Nearly a whole week.

Non-stop!

The river in the valley below Mr Strong's house had burst its banks and was flooding the meadows.

Mr Strong walked down the lane beneath the dripping trees.

It was not long before he met a very worried-looking Farmer Fields.

"Good morning," said Mr Strong. "What's the matter?"

"It's my sheep," said Farmer Fields. "They're stuck in the meadow surrounded by water. I can't get them out!"

"Let's go and see," said Mr Strong. "I might be able to help."

Poor Farmer Fields' sheep were indeed in trouble.

And the bit of dry land left for them to stand on was getting small-er by the minute as the flood water rose higher.

Mr Strong waded out to the little island in the middle of the meadow and then waded back carrying two sheep above his head.

"Oh, well done," said Farmer Fields. "The only problem is that there are ninety-eight sheep left out there and we'll run out of time before you've carried them all across!"

"Mmmm," said Mr Strong. "I fear you may be right, but I think I have an idea. Do you mind if I borrow your barn?"

Farmer Fields smiled.

And you are probably smiling if you have read the other story about Mr Strong.

But for those of you who have not read that Mr Strong story, I'll tell you what he did.

He picked up the barn (that's right, a whole barn!) and carried it across to the sheep.

Then he lifted all the sheep into the barn, counting them carefully as he did, so as not to leave any behind.

And then he picked up the barn with all ninety-eight sheep inside, and waded back to Farmer Fields.

"Oh, thank you," said Farmer Fields, once all his sheep were safely in the field at the top of the hill.

"Barns are very handy things to have lying around," chuckled Mr Strong, and went home.

That evening Mr Strong ate an enormous plateful of fried eggs and went to bed early ...

163

... and fell fast ASHEEP! HA! HA!

LITTLE MISS DOTTY
has a dotty day out

Little Miss Dotty is about
to have the dottiest ever day out
in Nonsenseland - with her dotty friends
Mr Nonsense and Mr Silly!

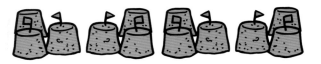

Little Miss Dotty

is every bit as dotty as her name suggests.

For instance, last year, Miss Dotty carpeted her garden path!

She lives in Nonsenseland, where the grass is blue and the trees are red, a place which is every bit as dotty as Miss Dotty.

In Nonsenseland all the pigs have televisions ...

... and wear slippers.

One day, while she was walking through Whoopee Wood, she met her two friends, Mr Silly and Mr Nonsense.

"Hello," said Miss Dotty.

"Hello," said Mr Silly and Mr Nonsense at the same time.

Mr Silly was carrying a saw.

"We're going to make a see-saw," said Mr Nonsense.
"Would you like to join in?"

"Yes, please," said Miss Dotty, who had been wondering what to do.

So the three of them set off.

They walked and they walked and they walked a long, long way until they came to the seaside.

But being Nonsenseland the sand wasn't yellow, it was pink.

When they got to the water's edge Mr Silly threw the saw in!

Have you ever heard of anything so silly?

"Brilliant," said Mr Nonsense.

"That's the best sea-saw ever," agreed Miss Dotty.

"What shall we do now?" said Mr Silly.

"Let's go for a paddle," suggested Miss Dotty.

So they went to the shop on the pier and each bought
a paddle!

"That was fun," said Mr Nonsense.

"What next?"

"Let's dig in the sand," said Mr Silly.

"Good idea," said Miss Dotty.

So they went down to the beach and dug a big hole ...

... and then filled it in!

171

"I did enjoy that," grinned Mr Nonsense.

"I'm hungry," said Miss Dotty. "What shall we eat?"

"Easy peasy," said Mr Nonsense, "Sandwiches!"

And I'm sure you can guess what they did next.

That's right!

They put sand between slices of buttered bread and ate sand sandwiches!

Can you imagine anything more dotty!

After lunch they drew in the sand ...

with crayons!

And they sunbathed ...

under umbrellas!

The sun was setting as they walked all the long way back to Miss Dotty's house and had supper together.

"We must do that again," said Miss Dotty.

"We must," agreed the other two.

And they got up from the table and went back to the beach!

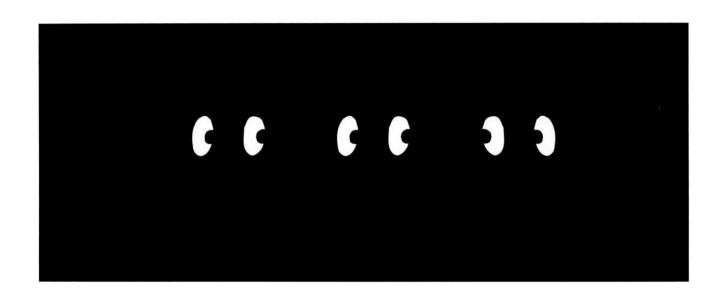

"It's dark, isn't it?" said Miss Dotty.

MR. TOPSY-TURVY
the round way wrong

Mr Topsy-Turvy likes doing things
the wrong way round -
so imagine what happens
when he decides to move house!

If Mr Topsy-Turvy can do something the wrong way round then you can be certain that he will.

Like the way he drives a car.

Which explains why you never see him driving a car ...

... and why he travels by bus.

Mr Topsy-Turvy woke up early one morning.

He has a very topsy-turvy way of sleeping in bed, as you can see.

He yawned and stretched and got up.

Then he went upstairs for breakfast.

That's right, Mr Topsy-Turvy's house is just as topsy-turvy as he is.

All his bedrooms are downstairs and his kitchen and living room are upstairs.

Mr Topsy-Turvy decided to have cornflakes for breakfast.

He opened the packet.

But being Mr Topsy-Turvy he didn't pour the cornflakes out, oh no, he poured the milk into the packet!

His meals tend to be very messy affairs.

After he had finished breakfast Mr Topsy-Turvy caught the bus into town. "One town for ticket, please," he said to the bus driver.

The bus driver scratched his head.

"Don't you mean, one ticket for town?" he said.

"Right that's," said Mr Topsy-Turvy.

Mr Topsy-Turvy speaks as topsy-turvily as everything else he does.

Now, this day was a rather special day for Mr Topsy-Turvy.
He had been saving up to buy a new house.

He went into Mr Homes' estate agency and said, "I'd like new
to house a buy."

Mr Homes knew Mr Topsy-Turvy quite well.

"You mean, you'd like to buy a new house?"

"Right that's," said Mr Topsy-Turvy, for the second time that day.

Mr. Homes

"If you wait outside the front I'll go and get my car," said Mr Homes.

And of course Mr Topsy-Turvy waited outside the back.

After Mr Homes eventually found him they set off in the car to look at some houses.

They looked at all sorts.

Tall, skinny houses.

Short, squat houses.

Even short, skinny houses, but Mr Topsy-Turvy didn't like any of them.

None of them seemed quite right to him.

As they were driving back to town Mr Topsy-Turvy suddenly shouted to Mr Homes to stop the car.

Well, what he actually said was, "Stop car the!" but Mr Homes knew what he meant.

On the other side of a hedge was the strangest house you have ever seen.

Everything was upside-down.

In fact, everything was topsy-turvy.

And I'm sure you can guess whose house it was.

"Now, house of that's the sort want I," said Mr Topsy-Turvy.

"But ... " said Mr Homes, "but that's your house!"

"Right that's," said Mr Topsy-Turvy, for the third time that day.

"But you can't move house into your own house!" exclaimed Mr Homes. "That would be all the round way wrong ... I mean the

wrong way round."

Mr Topsy-Turvy grinned a huge grin.

"Exactly," he said.

LITTLE MISS HELPFUL
and the green house

Little Miss Helpful loves to help.
So when Mr Slow says he wants
a greenhouse she decides
to make his dream come true!

With a name like Helpful

you would think that Little Miss Helpful
would be helpful, wouldn't you?

Well, you'd be wrong.

She wanted to help people more
than anything else in the world,
but as hard as she tried, she always
ended up being unhelpful.

One day, about a week ago, Little Miss Helpful was sitting on a bus on her way to town.

Mr Slow and Mr Happy were sitting in front of her having a conversation.

"I ... wish ... I ... had ... a ... green ... house ... but ... I ... never ... get ... the ... time ... to ... do ... anything," said Mr Slow to Mr Happy.

It was a very slow conversation.

Just then the bus stopped.

Now what Little
Miss Helpful had just
overheard had given her
an idea.

She got off the bus …

… and walked across to
Mr Nail's hardware
shop, and bought all the
green paint that he had.

Then Mr Nail delivered
all the green paint to …
Mr Slow's house.

I am sure you can guess what she had in mind.

That's right.

She was going to surprise Mr Slow by helping him paint his house green.

Helpful Little Miss Helpful!

Little Miss Helpful
started to paint.

She painted all
the walls.

She painted all
the doors.

194

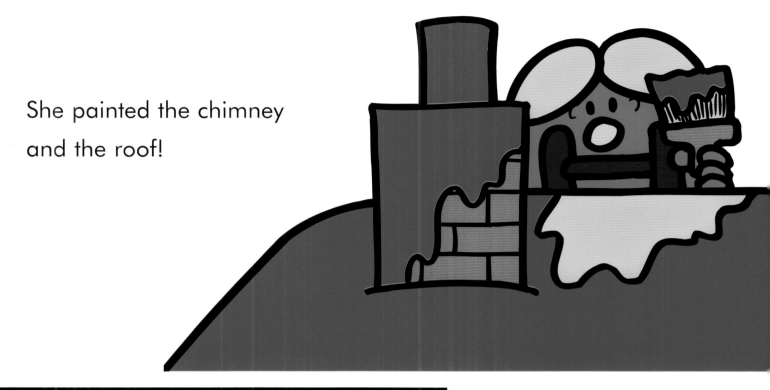

She painted the chimney
and the roof!

She even painted
all the windows.

The window
panes as well
as the frames!

195

When she had finished painting the house she still had some paint left over.

So she painted the garage as well.

Outside and inside!

Little Miss Helpful was terribly pleased with herself.

She stood back to admire her handiwork.

It was then that Mr Slow arrived back home.

In the time it had taken Miss Helpful to paint his house he had bought a loaf of bread.

He isn't called Mr Slow for nothing.

Mr Slow had to look twice before he realised that his house was still there.

"What ... have ... you ... done?" he exclaimed.

"You said that you wanted a green house," said Miss Helpful, "so there you are."

"That's ... not ... what ... I ... meant. I ... want ... a ... green-house," said Mr Slow.

"Exactly," said Miss Helpful. "And I painted your house green."

"No. I ... want ... the ... sort ... of ... greenhouse ... that ... you ... grow ... tomatoes ... in," explained Mr Slow, slowly.

"Oh ... " said Little Miss Helpful.

" … then what colour did you want your house to be?"

Mr Slow groaned a very slow groan. He could see it was going to be a very long afternoon.

Even for him!

MR. SMALL
a big day out

Mr Small is really very small indeed.

Imagine what would happen if

Mr Small suddenly became very big!

Mr Small was
out for a walk.

He was feeling more than a little sorry for himself.

It wasn't much fun being as small as he was.

He sat down under a tree and closed his eyes.

"I do so wish I was bigger," he sighed.

"Much, much bigger," he added.

Now, Mr Small did not know that there was a wizard lying down on the other side of the tree.

He had stopped for a snooze and, just as he had been dozing off, the wizard had overheard Mr Small's wish.

The wizard smiled to himself.

Without even opening his eyes, he muttered some magic words under his breath and then went back to sleep.

As Mr Small lay there, something really quite remarkable happened.

Something really quite remarkably magic.

Mr Small began to grow.

And grow.

And grow.

Until he bumped his head on a branch!

204

When he crawled out from underneath the tree and stood up he was taller than the tree.

Much taller.

"Gosh," said Mr Small.

He could not believe his eyes.

He could not believe his size!

He went for a walk to try out his new size.

It was wonderful.

He could see over the top of everything.

He leap-frogged over trees and jumped over rivers.

He gave Mr Uppity
the shock of his life.

He was stronger
than Mr Strong.

Noisier than

Mr Noisy.

And taller

than Mr Tall!

He could even make his fingers meet when he put his arms around Mr Greedy's tummy!

Mr Small had a marvellous day, and as the sun set he lay down in a field and went to sleep.

As Mr Small slept he shrank back to his normal size.

For you see, the wizard had only cast a spell that would last one day.

When Mr Small woke up it was dark.

"What a wonderful dream," he said to himself, and got up to walk home.

But he found he couldn't. He was surrounded by a wall!

However, when he felt along the bottom, he discovered that he could lift up the wall.

It was light outside, and when he crawled out Mr Small could not believe his eyes.

He had been trapped underneath a hat!

A hat that looked just like his own, but it was much, much bigger.

"Well, I never," said Mr Small. "Maybe it wasn't a dream after all."
That sleepy old wizard had forgotten to finish off his spell properly.

He had forgotten to make sure Mr Small's hat had shrunk back to
the right size.

Mr Small now had a ten-gallon hat.

A ten-gallon hat for a pint-sized person!

LITTLE MISS SPLENDID
and the house with a view

Little Miss Splendid's house has
a splendid view apart from
her un-splendid neighbour, Mr Mean!
But things are about to change…

Little Miss Splendid
looked out of her very
splendid window, set
in her most splendid
house, at her very
splendid garden,
and smiled.

And then she frowned.

Little Miss Splendid looked
out of her window every
morning and every
morning she smiled and
then she frowned.

And what made her frown?

I'll tell you.

214

At the bottom of her garden, on the other side of a small stream, lived Mr Mean.

Unlike Miss Splendid's very large and most splendid house, Mr Mean's house is very small and very run down.

A not at all splendid house.

In fact, the most un-splendid house one could ever imagine.

Mr Mean was the sort of person who did not like spending money, especially on his house.

Little Miss Splendid was the complete opposite.

And she did not like having Mr Mean as a neighbour.

His house quite ruined her splendid view.

It was on this particular morning as she stood looking out of

her window that Miss Splendid had an idea.

She rang her builder, Mr Trowel.

"Hello," she said, "this is Miss Splendid. I would like you to build a wall for me. Come at once."

Mr Trowel was over within an hour, and within a day he had built a wall at the bottom of Little Miss Splendid's garden.

A high wall.

A wall that hid Mr Mean's house.

Now, Mr Mean also liked to look out of his window each morning.

He had a splendid view of Miss Splendid's extraordinarily splendid house.

And what made the view all the more splendid for Mr Mean was the fact that it hadn't cost him a penny.

217

Mr Mean was very unhappy when he looked out of his window the next day and all he could see was a high, red brick wall.

But as he stood there looking out of his window Mr Mean had an idea.

The next morning when Little Miss Splendid looked out of the window she couldn't believe her eyes.

There was a huge hole in her beautiful wall and through the hole she could see Mr Mean's ramshackle house.

Miss Splendid was furious.

She rang Mr Trowel immediately and by lunchtime Mr Trowel had rebuilt the wall.

But the next morning there was another hole in her wall.

And so it went on all week.

Overnight, Mr Mean would knock a hole in the wall and the next day Mr Trowel would come and repair it.

And then one morning the whole wall had disappeared.

But not just the wall.

There was no sign of Mr Mean's house either!

"That's strange,"
said Miss Splendid to herself.
She put on her best hat and
went to investigate.

When she got down to where
Mr Mean's house had been
she heard the sound of
building coming from the
other side of the hill. She
climbed to the top of the hill.

And for the second
time she couldn't
believe her eyes.

There was Mr Busy
putting the finishing
touches to a house
that looked liked hers,
but was even
more splendid!

221

"Looks good, doesn't it?" said a voice behind her.

It was Mr Mean.

"What ... what ... how?" spluttered Miss Splendid.

"It was all those bricks that gave me the idea," said Mr Mean, and grinned. "All those free bricks!"

Little Miss Splendid didn't know what to say.

So she didn't say anything.

And she went home.

To her splendid house.

A splendid house, but no longer

the most splendid house!

MR. MISCHIEF
a spot of trouble

Mr Mischief thinks he has found
the perfect new way of
spreading some mischief!
But has he?

Mr Mischief woke up and groaned.

He did not feel well.

In fact, he felt decidedly unwell.

He got up and went to the bathroom to look at himself in the mirror.

He was covered in spots!

So he made an appointment with Dr Makeyouwell.

"You've got measles," said the Doctor, "and the best thing you can do is go home to bed and stay there for a week."

Mr Mischief's face fell.

A whole week in bed.

No mischief for a whole week!

Mr Mischief groaned for the second time that day.

"And don't forget," said Dr Makeyouwell as Mr Mischief was leaving, "measles are very catching."

Mr Mischief closed the door and then he grinned.

A very mischievous grin.

The sort of grin that meant that he was about to get up to no good.

Before he went home, Mr Mischief popped into the hardware shop and bought a pot of yellow paint.

Then he painted over all his spots, before paying Mr Happy a visit.

He didn't stay long, just long enough.

Long enough, thought Mr Mischief as he walked home, to give Mr Happy the measles!

When he got home he went to bed and lay there chuckling to himself. What a nasty person he is!

All the next day he lay in bed and thought about the trick he had played on Mr Happy.

And he thought, if Mr Happy had the measles, then Mr Tickle might catch them from Mr Happy.

Mr Mischief chuckled at the thought of Mr Tickle with spots all over his long arms.

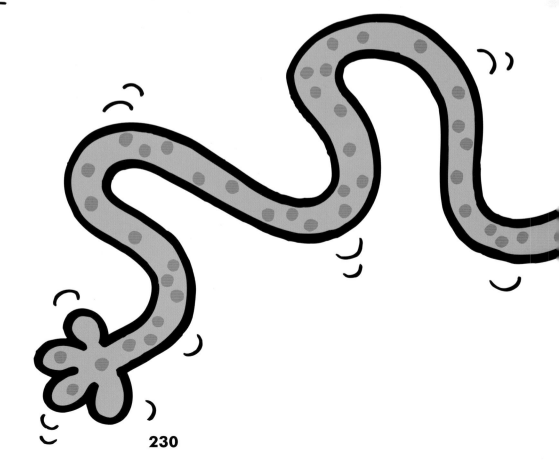

And Mr Nosey might catch the measles from Mr Tickle.

And he chuckled at the thought of Mr Nosey with a spotty nose.

And he chuckled at the thought of Mr Tall with spotty legs.

And Mr Wrong, who would probably have blue spots, because he gets everything wrong.

And Little Miss Tiny would only have room for one spot on her body.

"This will keep me happy all week long," chuckled Mr Mischief to himself.

Just then there was a knock at the door.

Mr Mischief struggled out of bed and answered it.

"Hello," said Mr Happy. "I heard you had the measles so I thought I'd come round and cheer you up. Here, I bought you these."

Mr Happy gave Mr Mischief a bunch of grapes.

Mr Mischief looked at Mr Happy, but as hard as he looked, he couldn't see any spots.

Not one!

"Aren't you afraid of catching the measles from me?" stammered Mr Mischief.

"Of course not," said Mr Happy, "I've already had them. And as you know, you can only get measles once!"

Mr Mischief's face fell and he groaned.

Again.

"What's wrong?" asked Mr Happy.

"Don't you like grapes?"

LITTLE MISS TINY
just the right size

Little Miss Tiny decides to explore.

Being small is lots of fun

but she soon finds herself

in big, big, trouble!

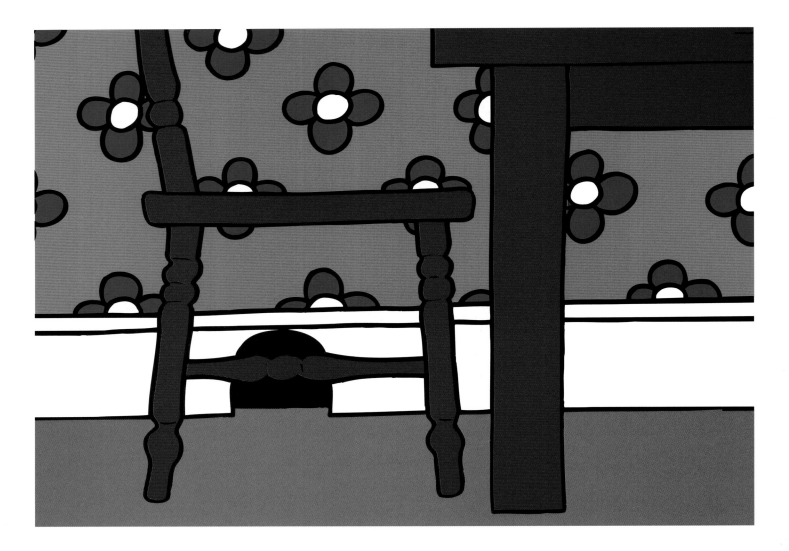

Little Miss Tiny lives in a mousehole in the dining-room of Home Farm.

One day she woke up early and decided to go exploring.

Exploring upstairs!

In all the time she had lived at Home Farm she had never been upstairs.

Well, when you are as small as Little Miss Tiny, a staircase is like a mountain.

Little Miss Tiny started to climb the stairs.

She climbed, and she climbed, and she climbed some more.

All the way to the top.

It took her nearly the whole morning!

Everything was very quiet because everyone had gone out for the day.

She wandered through the bedrooms.

She explored the bathroom.

239

And then she discovered the nursery.

Lying on the floor was a box with a hook on the lid.

She lifted the hook ...

... and got the fright of her life.

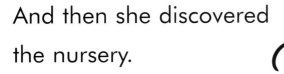

"Help!" she shrieked, and hid under the bed.

After a while she plucked up courage and peeked out.

"You silly-billy," she said to herself, "it's only a jack-in-the-box."

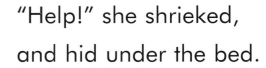

240

She began to
look around.

It was wonderful.

She said, "How do
you do," to a very
serious-looking soldier.

She tickled a
teddy bear.

And climbed a tower of blocks.

It was from the top of the blocks that Little Miss Tiny saw the most wonderful sight she had seen in all her tiny life.

A doll's house!

Little Miss Tiny opened the front door and went in.

Everything was just the right size for her.
The chairs, the table, the cups and even the stairs.

She went upstairs.

And lay down on the bed and closed her eyes.

She suddenly woke up with a start.

There, looking through the bedroom window of the doll's house, was the farm cat!

Little Miss Tiny didn't know what to do. How was she going to get back to her mousehole?

She went downstairs and through a door.

The farm cat watched her through the windows.

She found herself in a garage on the side of the doll's house, and in the garage was a wind-up toy car.

The little car gave her an idea.

She turned the key on the car, wound it up and jumped in.

The little car took off like a rocket through the little garage doors and straight through the cat's legs!

The car and Little Miss Tiny raced across the carpet, out through the door and down the landing.

Little Miss Tiny laughed with glee.

And then realised she had laughed too soon.

The car shot over the top step of the stairs and out into space and down …

and down …

and down …

Little Miss Tiny shrieked.

With a SPLASH! she landed in the cat's bowl of milk at the bottom of the stairs.

She rushed through the hall, ran across the dining-room floor and back to the safety of her mousehole.

"Phew! That was close!" she said, with a big sigh of relief.

Well, a big sigh of relief

for someone as tiny as Little Miss Tiny.